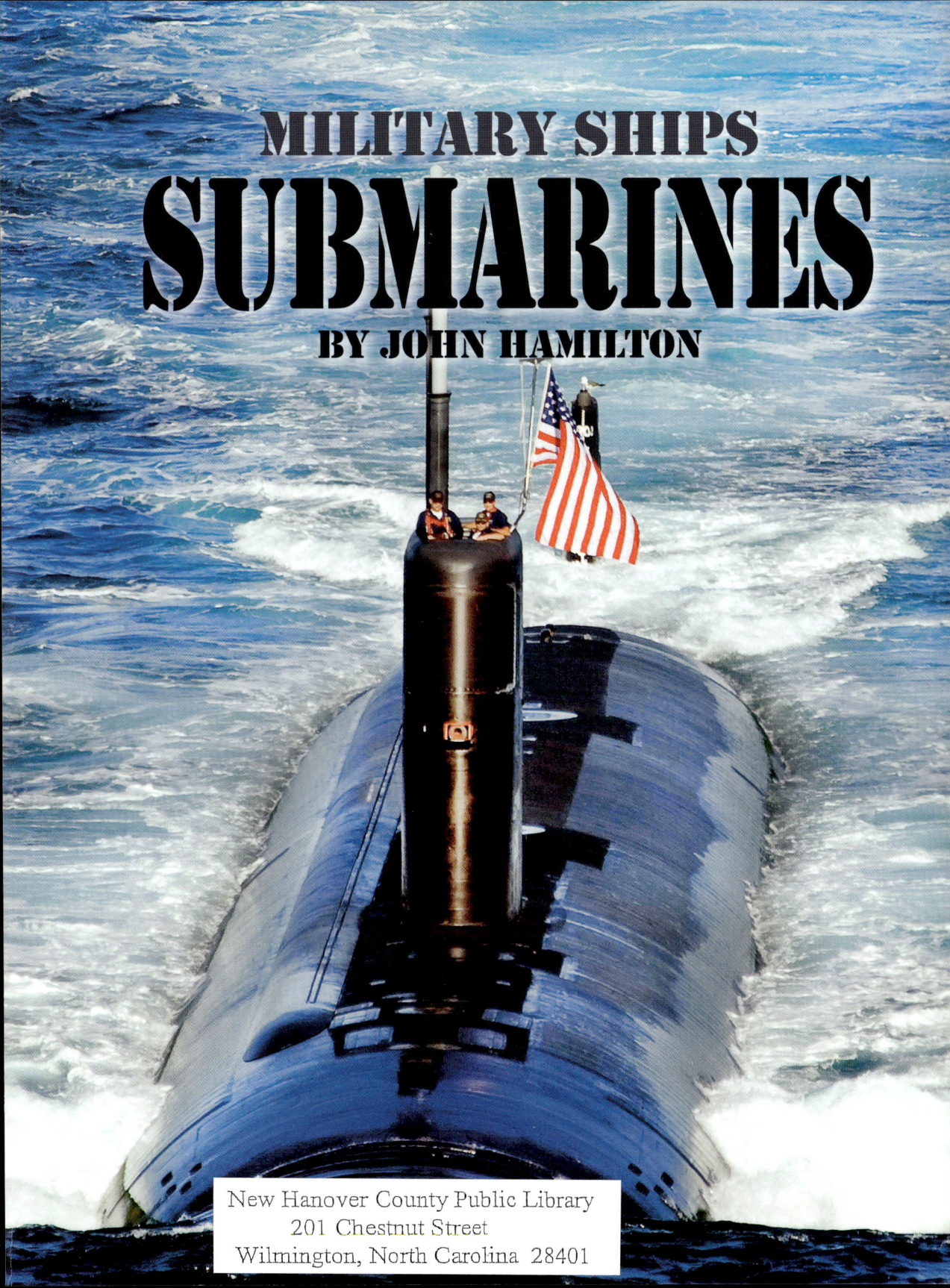

MILITARY SHIPS
SUBMARINES
BY JOHN HAMILTON

New Hanover County Public Library
201 Chestnut Street
Wilmington, North Carolina 28401

VISIT US AT
WWW.ABDOPUBLISHING.COM

Published by ABDO Publishing Company, PO Box 398166, Minneapolis, MN 55439. Copyright ©2013 by Abdo Consulting Group, Inc. International copyrights reserved in all countries. No part of this book may be reproduced in any form without written permission from the publisher. A&D Xtreme™ is a trademark and logo of ABDO Publishing Company.

Printed in the United States of America, North Mankato, Minnesota.
032012
092012

 PRINTED ON RECYCLED PAPER

Editor: Sue Hamilton
Graphic Design: Sue Hamilton
Cover Design: John Hamilton
Cover Photo: United States Navy
Interior Photos: All photos United States Navy except AP-pg 6; Huntington Ingalls Industries-pgs 4-5, 8-9 & 10-11; National Archives-pg 7; Thinkstock-pg 5 (inset).

ABDO Booklinks
Web sites about Military Ships are featured on our Book Links pages. These links are routinely monitored and updated to provide the most current information available.
Web site: www.abdopublishing.com

Library of Congress Cataloging-in-Publication Data

Hamilton, John, 1959-
  Submarines / John Hamilton.
      p. cm.
   Includes index.
   ISBN 978-1-61783-524-7
   1. Submarines (Ships)--Juvenile literature. I. Title.
  VM365.H237 2012
  623.825'7--dc23
                                2012005071

TABLE OF CONTENTS

Submarines 4
History 6
Construction 8
Propulsion 10
Crew 12
Attack Submarines 14
Attack Submarines Fast Facts 16
Fleet Ballistic Missile Submarines 22
Fleet Ballistic Missile Submarines Fast Facts 24
Guided Missile Submarines 26
Guided Missile Submarines Fast Facts 28
Glossary 30
Index 32

SUBMARINES

Submarines are one of the most important kinds of vessels in the United States Navy. They use the element of surprise. They can stay submerged under the sea for weeks, or even months. They can travel in deep water, undetected by the enemy.

Submarines carry many kinds of weapons. Torpedoes are effective against enemy vessels. Cruise missiles can strike targets far inland. Some U.S. Navy subs are armed with nuclear missiles. These powerful weapons can destroy targets anywhere on Earth.

XTREME FACT

Submarines use sonar. It is a system that analyzes sound waves traveling through water to find enemy vessels or underwater obstacles.

HISTORY

The Turtle *was developed by inventor David Bushnell in 1776. It had an oak hull and a brass conning tower/hatch.*

Submarines have been used in warfare as early as the Revolutionary War. In 1776, the *Turtle* became the first submarine used in combat. During the American Civil War, the Confederate submarine *H.L. Hunley* sank a Union ship in Charleston Harbor, South Carolina. These early vessels were not very effective. They were also dangerous to their crews.

On February 17, 1864, the Confederate submarine H.L. Hunley *sank the Union ship USS* Housatonic.

Submarines were used by several countries during World War I and World War II, especially the United States, Germany, and Japan. During the Cold War, from 1945 to 1991, new technology allowed submarines to carry nuclear missiles, and to stay submerged for long periods of time.

A torpedoed Japanese destroyer, as seen through the periscope of the USS Nautilus *in June 1942.*

A Navy officer looking through a periscope in the control room of a submarine in 1942.

XTREME FACT

During World War II, American submarines inflicted more than half of all Japanese merchant shipping losses.

CONSTRUCTION

Navy submarines are built in shipyards in Newport News, Virginia, and Groton, Connecticut. Modern military submarines are constructed in parts called modules. Finished modules are brought together on a rail system and welded together.

XTREME FACT

The sail is the top-most part of a submarine. It looks like a small tower. It holds periscopes, plus communications and radar masts. Some sails also have diving planes. These wing-like structures help the submarine steer.

A nearly completed USS Texas awaiting its launch in 2005.

A submarine's outer shell is called the pressure hull. It is made of extremely strong steel. This allows submarines to withstand the tremendous pressures of deep water.

PROPULSION

United States Navy military submarines are nuclear powered. A heavily shielded nuclear reactor is in the middle of the ship. It generates heat that turns water to steam. Steam power turns a shaft in the rear of the ship. A propeller is on the end of the shaft. It spins in the water, propelling the submarine.

XTREME FACT

In the Navy, propellers are known as screws. On modern submarines, they are high-tech pieces of equipment, shrouded in secrecy. They allow submarines to travel quietly through the water.

In addition to propulsion, a submarine's nuclear generator provides power to maintain clean air and other life-support systems for the crew.

The USS North Carolina *attack submarine under construction in 2007. The propeller is covered to keep the technology secret.*

CREW

Submarine crew members are specially selected volunteers. These "submariners" live together in cramped spaces. They are cut off from the rest of the world, sometimes for months at a time. They undergo tests to make sure they can handle the stresses of undersea living. They are all highly skilled in their jobs.

Submariners catching up before getting underway on board the USS Virginia.

Submariners wear blue, lint-free coveralls (lint clogs the ship's air purifiers). They also wear non-slip shoes, like tennis shoes. Rubber-soled shoes are quiet. This is important in order to avoid detection by enemy sonar.

XTREME FACT

In the past, because of close quarters and long sea missions, no women were allowed to serve on U.S. Navy submarines. However, starting in 2012, the first women sailors began serving on the Navy's large ballistic missile and guided missile submarines.

ATTACK SUBMARINES

The United States Navy has two main groups of military submarines. They include large vessels that carry long-range missiles, and fast attack submarines. Attack submarines are smaller. They are designed to seek out and destroy enemy vessels, including other submarines. They are armed with torpedoes and cruise missiles.

Navy SEALs fast roping from a Seahawk helicopter to the hull of the fast attack submarine USS Hampton.

XTREME FACT

U.S. Navy subs use Mk-48 torpedoes, which are designed to sink "fast, deep-diving nuclear subs" or surface ships. They have an official range of greater than five miles (8 km).

Attack submarines also spy on enemy forces and protect aircraft carrier battle groups. They can carry special operations forces, usually Navy SEALs. Using underwater gear, these forces can be secretly dropped off in hostile coastal areas.

ATTACK SUBMARINES FAST FACTS

There are three classes of attack submarines in today's U.S. Navy. The Los Angeles-class vessels are the backbone of the Navy's submarine force. There are currently 43 in service.

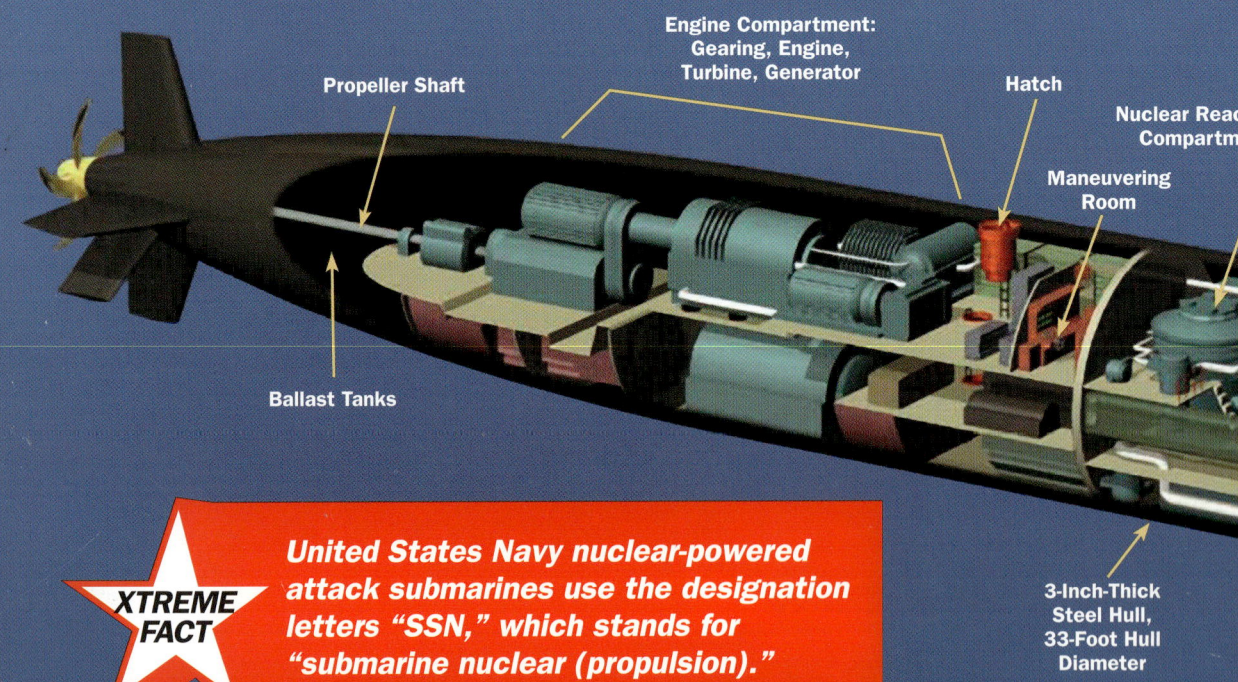

Engine Compartment: Gearing, Engine, Turbine, Generator
Propeller Shaft
Hatch
Nuclear Reactor Compartment
Maneuvering Room
Ballast Tanks
3-Inch-Thick Steel Hull, 33-Foot Hull Diameter

XTREME FACT: United States Navy nuclear-powered attack submarines use the designation letters "SSN," which stands for "submarine nuclear (propulsion)."

Los Angeles-Class Specifications

Length:	360 feet (110 m)
Width (beam):	33 feet (10 m)
Displacement:	7,728 tons (7,011 metric tons)
Propulsion:	One nuclear reactor, one shaft
Speed (submerged):	25-plus knots (29+ mph/46+ kph)
Normal Maximum Depth (test depth):	950 feet (290 m)
Crew:	16 officers, 127 enlisted
Armament:	Tomahawk cruise missiles, Mk-48 torpedoes (four torpedo tubes)

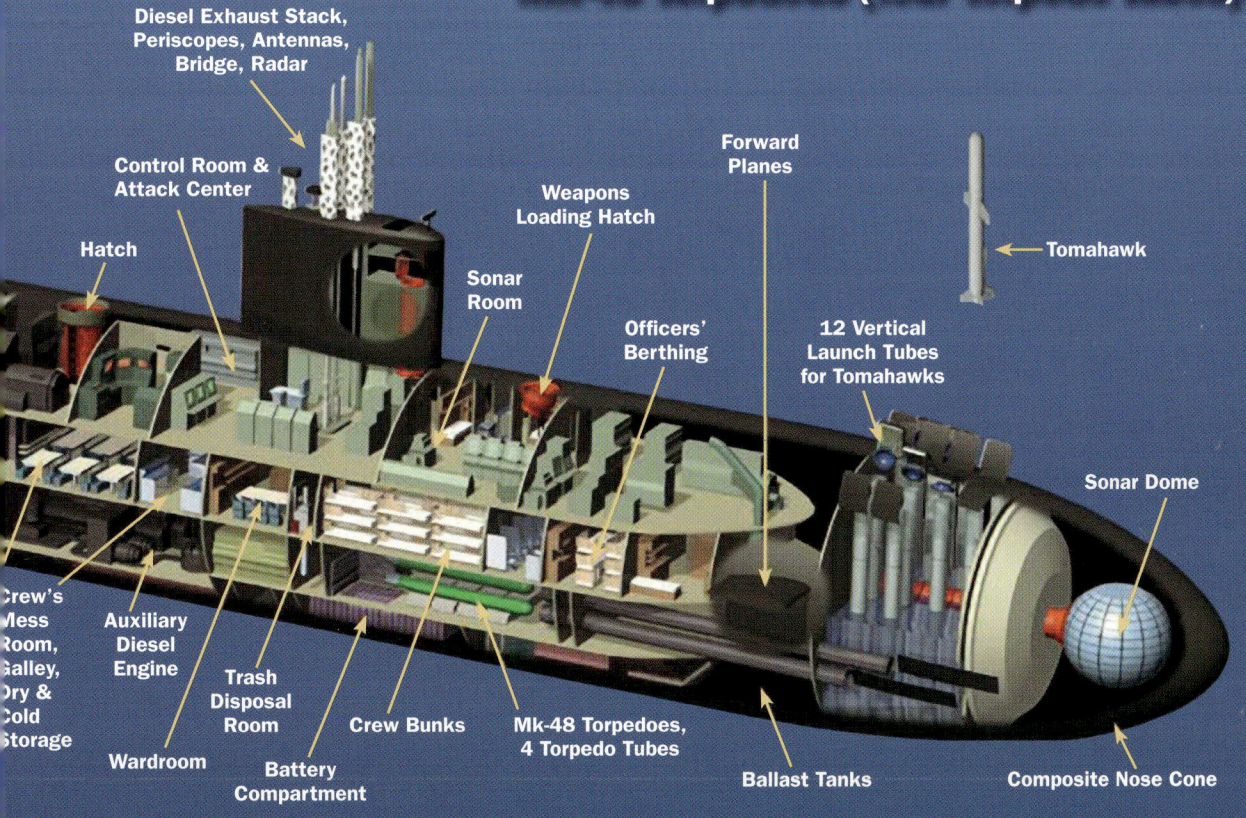

Seawolf-Class Specifications

Length:	353 feet (108 m)
Width (beam):	40 feet (12 m)
Displacement:	10,234 tons (9,284 metric tons)
Propulsion:	One nuclear reactor, one shaft
Speed (submerged):	25-plus knots (29+ mph/46+ kph)
Normal Maximum Depth (test depth):	2,000 feet (610 m)
Crew:	14 officers, 126 enlisted
Armament:	Tomahawk cruise missiles, Mk-48 torpedoes (eight torpedo tubes)

XTREME FACT — Budget constraints and the end of the Cold War in 1991 resulted in the construction of just three Seawolf-class submarines.

Seawolf-class attack submarines are built to be quiet and fast. They are also well armed. The torpedo room can hold up to 50 weapons. These attack subs have advanced sensors and may be used to carry out classified research.

The USS Connecticut *surfacing through Arctic Ocean ice to support on-going research in the area.*

Virginia-Class Specifications

Length: 377 feet (115 m)
Width (beam): 33 feet (10 m)
Displacement: 8,736 tons (7,925 metric tons)
Propulsion: One nuclear reactor, one shaft
Speed (submerged): 25-plus knots (29+ mph/46+ kph)
Normal Maximum Depth (test depth): 800 feet (244 m)
Crew: 15 officers, 117 enlisted
Armament: Tomahawk cruise missiles (12 vertical launch system tubes), Mk-48 torpedoes (four torpedo tubes)

Virginia-class submarines are the newest in the U.S. Navy's submarine fleet. They have advanced electronics, communications, and a quieter propulsion system. They will eventually replace older Los Angeles-class submarines.

A Seahawk helicopter flying alongside the Virginia-class attack submarine USS *New Mexico.*

FLEET BALLISTIC MISSILE SUBMARINES

Fleet ballistic missile submarines are the most powerful weapons on earth. They are nicknamed "Boomers," and are the largest submarines in the U.S. Navy's fleet.

The fleet ballistic missile submarine USS Alaska *returning to its homeport.*

A test launching of an unarmed Trident II missile from the fleet ballistic missile submarine USS Nevada.

Boomers carry up to 24 ballistic missiles. Each missile has several warheads. The vessels stay submerged for months. Potential enemies never know exactly where they are. If enemies attack the United States, they risk nuclear destruction from Navy submarines. This fear of retaliation is called "deterrence." It prevents enemies from attacking the United States.

XTREME FACT

Boomers are armed with Trident II missiles. They are launched while the submarine is submerged. The missiles have a range of about 7,000 miles (11,265 km).

FLEET BALLISTIC MISSILE SUBMARINES FAST FACTS

United States Navy nuclear-powered ballistic missile submarines use the designation letters "SSBN," which stands for "Submarine Ballistic (missile) Nuclear (propulsion)."

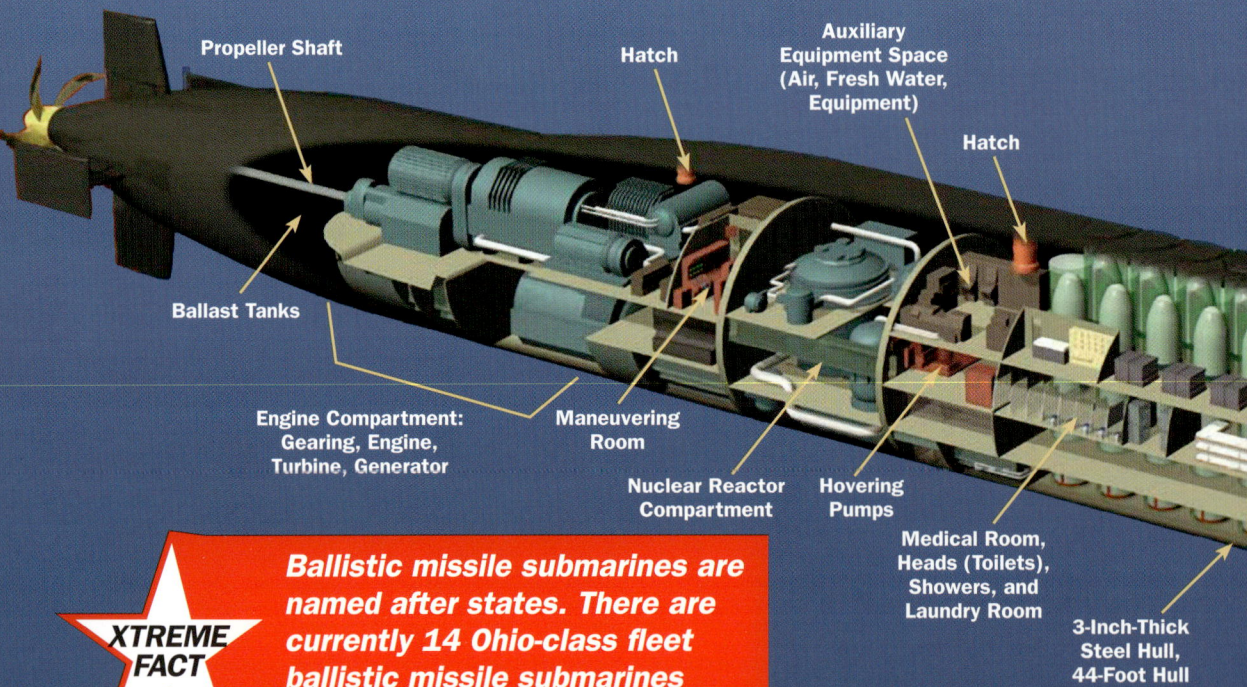

- Propeller Shaft
- Hatch
- Auxiliary Equipment Space (Air, Fresh Water, Equipment)
- Hatch
- Ballast Tanks
- Engine Compartment: Gearing, Engine, Turbine, Generator
- Maneuvering Room
- Nuclear Reactor Compartment
- Hovering Pumps
- Medical Room, Heads (Toilets), Showers, and Laundry Room
- 3-Inch-Thick Steel Hull, 44-Foot Hull Diameter

XTREME FACT: Ballistic missile submarines are named after states. There are currently 14 Ohio-class fleet ballistic missile submarines in service.

Ohio-Class Specifications

Length: 560 feet (171 m)
Width (beam): 42 feet (13 m)
Displacement: 18,776 tons (17,033 metric tons)
Propulsion: One nuclear reactor, one shaft
Speed (submerged): 20-plus knots (23+ mph/37+ kph)
Normal Maximum Depth (test depth): 800 feet (244 m)
Crew: 15 officers, 140 enlisted
Armament: 24 Trident II ballistic missiles, Mk-48 torpedoes (four torpedo tubes)

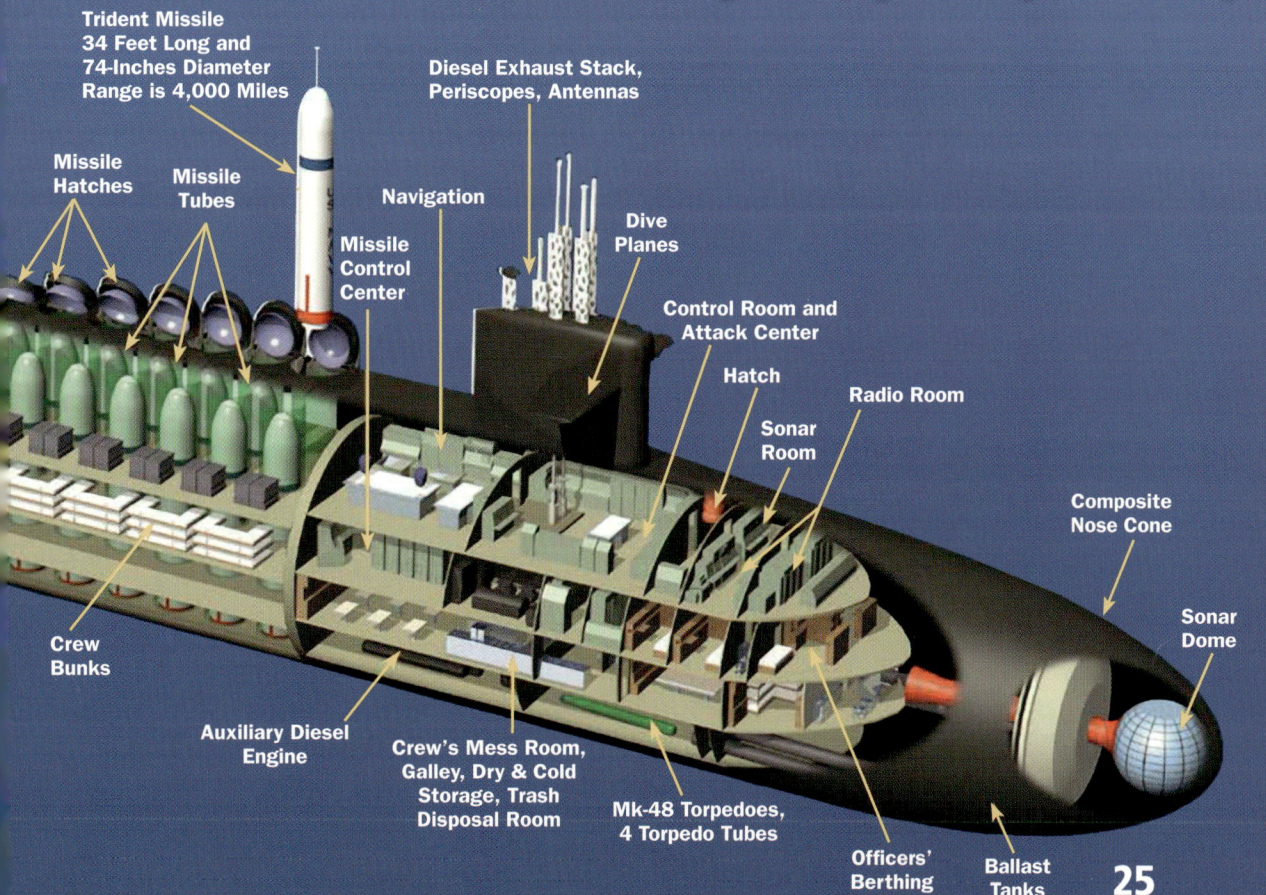

GUIDED MISSILE SUBMARINES

In recent years, four Ohio-class SSBN ballistic missile submarines have been converted into SSGN guided missile submarines.

The ballistic nuclear missiles have been removed. In their place, the submarines now carry up to 154 Tomahawk cruise missiles. Ohio-class guided missile submarines are also big enough to carry up to 66 special operations personnel, such as Navy SEALs.

The Ohio-class guided missile submarine USS Florida making a routine visit to Greece.

XTREME FACT
Two nuclear missile tubes on each guided missile submarine were converted to allow special operations troops to leave and enter the submarine without the vessel needing to surface.

GUIDED MISSILE SUBMARINES FAST FACTS

Ohio-Class Specifications

Length:	560 feet (171 m)
Width (beam):	42 feet (13 m)
Displacement:	18,776 tons (17,033 metric tons)
Propulsion:	One nuclear reactor, one shaft
Speed (submerged):	20-plus knots (23+ mph/37+ kph)
Normal Maximum Depth (test depth):	800 feet (244 m)
Crew:	15 officers, 144 enlisted
Armament:	Up to 154 Tomahawk missiles, Mk-48 torpedoes (four torpedo tubes)

XTREME FACT: There are currently four Ohio-class guided missile submarines in service: the USS Ohio, USS Michigan, USS Florida, and USS Georgia.

GLOSSARY

Ballistic
An object, such as a ballistic missile, that begins with a powered upwards momentum, and then free-falls in a mathematically calculated path guided by gravity as it approaches its target.

Cold War
The Cold War was a time of political, economic, and cultural tension between the United States and its allies and the Soviet Union and other Communist nations. It lasted from about 1947, just after the end of World War II, until the early 1990s, when the Soviet Union collapsed and Communism was no longer a major threat to the United States.

Deter
To prevent or discourage an action from occurring.

Displacement
Displacement is a way of measuring a ship's mass, or size. It equals the weight of the water a ship displaces, or occupies, while floating. Think of a bathtub filled to the rim with water. A toy boat placed in the tub would cause water to spill over the sides. The weight of that water equals the weight of the boat.

Hull
The main body of a ship. It includes the bottom, sides and deck.

Radar
A way to detect objects, such as aircraft or ships, using electromagnetic (radio) waves. Radar waves are sent out by large dishes, or antennas, and then strike an object. The radar dish then detects the reflected wave, which can tell operators how big an object is, how fast it is moving, its altitude, and its direction.

Sonar
Technology that allows ships and submarines to detect objects underwater by measuring sound waves. An "active sonar" system sends out a burst of sound, a "ping" that travels through the water. When the sound wave hits an object, such as a ship or underwater obstacle, the wave is reflected back. By measuring the reflected wave, sonar operators can determine the object's size, distance, and heading. "Passive sonar" detects the natural vibrations of objects in water. It is most often used by submarines, because sending out an active sonar signal might give away the submarine's position.

Tomahawk Cruise Missile
A missile that can be launched from a submerged submarine, as well as a ship, or aircraft. It has stubby wings, and can be used over medium- to long-range distances.

Warhead
The forward section of a bomb or missile usually containing an explosive charge. Warheads can also be filled with chemical or biological agents.

INDEX

A
Alaska, USS 22
Arctic Ocean 19

B
Boomers 22, 23
Bushnell, David 6

C
Charleston Harbor 6
Civil War 6
Cold War 7, 18
Connecticut 8
Connecticut, USS 19

E
Earth 5

F
Florida, USS 27, 29

G
Georgia, USS 29
Germany 7
Greece 27
Groton, CT

H
Hampton, USS 14
Housatonic, USS 6
Hunley, H.L. (submarine) 6

J
Japan 7

L
Los Angeles-class
   submarines 16, 17, 21

M
Michigan, USS 29
Mk-48 torpedo 15, 17,
   18, 20, 25, 28

N
Nautilus, USS 7
Navy, U.S. 4, 5, 7, 10,
   13, 14, 15, 16, 21,
   22, 23, 24, 27
Nevada, USS 23
New Mexico, USS 21
Newport News, VA
North Carolina, USS 11

O
Ohio, USS 29
Ohio-class submarines
   24, 25, 26, 27, 28, 29

R
Revolutionary War 6

S
Seahawk helicopter 14,
   21
Seawolf-class
   submarines 18, 19
SEALs, Navy 14, 15, 27
South Carolina 6
SSBN 24, 26
SSGN 26
SSN 16

T
Texas, USS 9
Tomahawk cruise
   missile 17, 18, 20,
   27, 28
Trident II missile 23, 25
Turtle (submersible) 6

U
United States 4, 5, 7,
   13, 14, 15, 16, 21,
   22, 23, 24

V
Virginia 8
Virginia, USS 13
Virginia-class
   submarines 20, 21

W
World War I 7
World War II 7

ML   3-13